Paddington at the Circus

PADDINGTON AT THE CIRCUS
Text copyright © 1972 by Michael Bond
Illustrations copyright © 1992 by HarperCollins Publishers, Ltd.
First published in Great Britain by William Collins Sons and Co Ltd.
This edition published in 1992 by HarperCollins Publishers Ltd.
Printed and bound in Great Britain
by BPCC Paulton Books
1   2   3   4   5   6   7   8   9   10
First American Edition, 1992

Library of Congress Cataloging-in-Publication Data
Bond, Michael.
    Paddington at the circus / Michael Bond ; illustrated by John Lobban.
        p.   cm.
    Summary: Paddington Bear and the Brown family go to the
circus, where Paddington ends up as part of the trapeze act.
    ISBN 0-694-00415-4.
    [1. Circus—Fiction.   2. Bears—Fiction.]   I. Lobban, John, ill.
II. Title.
PZ7.B6368Pacd   1992   91-44210
[E]—dc20   CIP
                                                    AC

Paddington at the Circus

Michael Bond

Illustrated by John Lobban

HarperFestival
A Division of HarperCollins*Publishers*

One day Paddington was out doing his morning shopping when he came across a very strange-looking man hanging a poster on a wall.

It showed a huge tent decorated with red and green and blue lights and streamers. Across the middle were the words THE GREATEST SHOW ON EARTH. ONE NIGHT ONLY. BOOK NOW.

When Paddington got home, he hurried inside to tell the others.

"The Greatest Show on Earth?" repeated Jonathan, giving Judy a wink. "In a *tent*? You must have been dreaming!"

Then Judy announced the good news. It was a circus, and they all had tickets for the front row that very evening.

Paddington had never been to a circus before, and he got more and more excited as the time drew near.

The lights were already on when they arrived, and there was a wonderful smell of sawdust in the air. The tent looked very festive and inviting.

The show itself was even more exciting.

There was a band, and a ringmaster in a top hat, and even a lady selling ice cream. There was so much to see that Paddington didn't know what to look at first.

"I think I would like to join a circus, Mr. Brown," he announced happily.

Then he caught sight of the man he had seen that morning. He was in the middle of the ring, balancing a bucket on the end of a long pole.

"That's a clown," explained Judy. "He's standing on stilts. That's why he looks so tall."

Paddington waved, and the man came over and bent down to shake his paw. The bucket tipped, and Paddington jumped up in alarm.

Luckily the bucket was empty and was tied to the end of the pole, so Paddington wasn't scared for long.

Mr. Brown bought him an ice cream, and as the band started to play, they all sat back to enjoy the show. All, that is, except Paddington.

The first act was hardly over when he had yet another shock. Looking up toward the roof of the tent,
he saw a man hanging from a rope.

"That must be one of the Popular Prices," began
Jonathan, looking at the program. "They're trapeze
artists—"

But Paddington didn't stop to listen. "Don't worry,
Mr. Price, I'm coming!"

Before the others could stop him, Paddington was halfway up the nearest tent pole.

He climbed onto a small platform, then almost fell off again when he saw a second man coming toward him.

The man was dressed in tights and was riding a bicycle.

But Paddington was not nearly as surprised as the men themselves.

"Look out!" shouted the leader. "Hold on!"

Paddington did as he was told. He grabbed the nearest thing he could see.

It came loose in his paw, and the next thing he knew, he was flying through the air.

The audience had been clapping before; but when Paddington appeared, they clapped more loudly than ever because they all thought he was part of the act.

He missed the platform on the other side and began to swing backward and forward, getting lower and lower, until he came to a stop over the middle of the ring.

"Don't let go!" shouted the ringmaster. "Whatever you do—don't let go!"

A look of horror came over the ringmaster's face as something soft and white landed on his beautifully clean top hat.

"Yikes!" exclaimed Jonathan. "Paddington's ice cream!"

In the end it was Paddington's friend the clown who saved him.

He balanced the bucket on the end of his pole so that Paddington could step into it.

As Paddington landed in the ring, the cheers from the crowd made the whole tent shake.

"Best act I've seen in years!" shouted a man near the Browns. "More! More!"

Paddington gave the man a hard stare as he stepped out of the bucket.

He'd had just about enough of being a trapeze artist for one night.

Even the ringmaster had to admit that Paddington had been the star attraction of the evening, and at the end of the show he gave Paddington another ice cream and insisted he take part in the Grand Parade.

"It's a pity we're only here for one night," the ringmaster said sadly. "I'd like to have you in my circus all the time."

"Do you still want to join a circus, Paddington?" asked Judy later that night.

Paddington shook his head. And then a faraway look came into his eyes as he tested his sheets carefully to make sure he was safely tucked in.

"But it was *very* nice to be asked," he said. "I don't suppose there are many bears from Darkest Peru who can say they've been on a trapeze!"